Anonymous

Cincinaty Industrial Exposition

Anatiposi

Anonymous

Cincinaty Industrial Exposition

Reprint of the original, first published in 1872.

1st Edition 2023 | ISBN: 978-3-38214-804-1

Anatiposi Verlag is an imprint of Outlook Verlagsgesellschaft mbH.

Verlag (Publisher): Outlook Verlag GmbH, Zeilweg 44, 60439 Frankfurt, Deutschland
Vertretungsberechtigt (Authorized to represent): E. Roepke, Zeilweg 44, 60439 Frankfurt, Deutschland
Druck (Print): Books on Demand GmbH, In de Tarpen 42, 22848 Norderstedt, Deutschland

Cincinnati

Industrial Exposition

OF

Manufactures, Products and the Arts.

RULES AND REGULATIONS

AND

Premium List

FOR THE

Third Exposition.

1872.

CINCINNATI:
ROBERT CLARKE & CO., Print.
1872.

THE THIRD

Cincinnati Industrial Exposition,

UNDER THE DIRECTION OF THE

BOARD OF COMMISSIONERS,

APPOINTED BY THE

Chamber of Commerce, Board of Trade, and Ohio Mechanics Institute,

WILL OPEN TO THE PUBLIC ON

WEDNESDAY, SEPTEMBER 4,

AND CONTINUE UNTIL

SATURDAY, OCTOBER 5,

1872.

Cincinnati Industrial Exposition,

1872.

Board of Commissioners.

Chamber of Commerce.

C. W. Rowland.
Lewis Seasongood.
George Sharples.
W. W. Taylor.
L. C. Weir.

Board of Trade.

A. T. Goshorn,
D. B. Pierson.
Clement Olhaber.
W. H. Blymyer.
Thomas G. Smith.

Ohio Mechanics Institute.

Thomas Gilpin.
H. McCollum.
James Dale.
Frank Millward.
A. L. Helm.

OFFICERS

STANDING COMMITTEES,

CINCINNATI INDUSTRIAL EXPOSITION,

1872.

FINANCE.

LEWIS SEASONGOOD,   R. R. SPRINGER,
J. SIMPKINSON,   A. P. C. BONTE,
JAMES BRADFORD,   GEORGE W. JONES.

BUILDING.

D. B. PIERSON,   H. McCOLLUM,
GEORGE SHARPLES.

RULES AND REGULATIONS.

H. McCOLLUM,   A. T. GOSHORN,
FRANK MILLWARD.

PRINTING AND ADVERTISING.

W. W. TAYLOR,   W. H. BLYMYER,
A. L. HELM.

TRANSPORTATION.

L. C. WEIR,   W. J. ARMEL,
F. A. ARMSTRONG.

PRIVILEGES.

CLEMENT OLHABER,   A. T. GOSHORN,
L. C. WEIR.

AWARDS.

THOMAS GILPIN,   H. McCOLLUM,
JAMES M. CLARK.

JUDGES.

JAMES DALE,   THOMAS GILPIN,
L. C. WEIR.

SPACE.

W. H. BLYMYER,   L. M. DAYTON,
THOMAS G. SMITH.

MACHINERY.

FRANK MILLWARD,   CHARLES A. WILSON.
GEORGE A. GRAY.

AGRICULTURAL DEPARTMENT.

W. H. BLYMYER,   THOMAS H. FOULDS,
R. H. LYMAN.

TEXTILE FABRICS.

THOMAS G. SMITH,   M. T. ANTRAM,
JOHN SHILLITO,   J. HEBERD,
EARL W. STIMSON,

LADIES DEPARTMENT.

C. W. ROWLAND,   W. P. ANDERSON,
LEWIS E. MILLS.

NATURAL HISTORY DEPARTMENT.

A. L. HELM,   DR. J. S. NEWBERRY,
L. S. COTTON,   JULIUS DEXTER,
DR. H. H. HILL.

FINE ARTS DEPARTMENT.

GEORGE SHARPLES,   JOHN R. TAIT,
P. H. BURT.

HORTICULTURAL DEPARTMENT.

CLEMENT OLHABER,   WILLIAM S. MUNSON,
L. C. WEIR,   ALEXANDER GORDON,
WILLIAM E. JONES.

COTTON.

C. W. ROWLAND,   GEORGE SHARPLES,
W. W. TAYLOR.

THIRD

Cincinnati Industrial Exposition,

1872.

The Board of Commissioners, in announcing the Third Grand Exposition, cordially invite from all sources contributions of works of art, new inventions, the products of the soil and mine, and of skilled labor in every branch of industry. They solicit the co-operation of those interested in their effort to attain variety and completeness, and to present the best works in every department.

Space Accommodations.

Profiting by the experience of former years, the management have matured plans for new buildings surpassing in extent any heretofore erected in the United States for a similar purpose, and comprising an exhibiting space of about 7 acres. In the arrangement of the various departments the convenience of both exhibitors and visitors has been carefully consulted, and an improved distribution of articles into groups will add largely to the general symmetry of the Exposition.

The want of a detached building for the Fine Arts' Department having been generally expressed, the management have erected for its use a handsome fire-proof structure, 62 by

160 feet, in the beautiful park opposite the main buildings, with which it is connected by an ornamental covered bridge across the intervening street.

Premium List.

Attention is called to the enlargement and thorough revision of the premium list, and to the special announcements in the Departments of Fine Arts, Natural History, and Horticulture.

Transportation.

Articles not sold during the Exposition will, as usual, be returned free by the transportation lines, and the new arrangements for reduced fares and excursion trains will insure a large increase in the number of visitors.

Hotel Accommodations.

The hotel accommodations of Cincinnati, heretofore ample, will be greatly enlarged in view of the increasing number of visitors which the Exposition attracts from all parts of the country, so that no deficiency in this respect may be feared.

Early Application.

Persons intending to exhibit at this Exposition should give early notice of the articles, and amount and kind of space required. Special attention is directed to the time for making application as required by the accompanying rules.

For further information address the *Secretary of the Cincinnati Industrial Exposition, Cincinnati.*

A. T. GOSHORN, *President.*

W. W. TAYLOR, *Secretary.*

THIRD

Cincinnati Industrial Exposition

1872.

RULES AND REGULATIONS.

The following Rules will be strictly adhered to and enforced:

I.

The halls and grounds will be open for the reception of articles from Wednesday, August 14th, to Saturday, August 31st. On Wednesday, September 4th, the Exposition will be opened to the public, and will continue open from day to day (Sundays excepted), from nine o'clock A. M. to ten o'clock P. M., until Saturday evening, October 5th.

II.

All articles will be entered for exhibition only, except those specifically named in the published list of articles to which premiums will be awarded; articles named in the premium list may be entered for exhibition or competition at the option of the exhibitor, which must not be later than August 31st.

III.

Articles intended for competition must be entered on the books as such not later than August 31st; otherwise they will be entered for exhibition only, and all articles must be in position ready for exhibition by Tuesday, September 3d. The driving engines will be in operation one week previous to the opening of the Exposition to the public, and exhibitors of machinery in motion will be required to have their machines in running order on the day of opening.

IV.

Each exhibitor (except in the Ladies' Department) will be required to pay an entry fee of two dollars. An exhibitor competing for more than one premium shall pay two dollars for each additional premium competed for.

Each exhibitor will have the privilege, upon payment of two dollars in addition to the entry fee for his articles, of securing a ticket of admission (positively not transferable) which will admit him at all hours of the Exposition. Not more than two exhibitors' admission tickets will be issued to a firm or corporation.

Ladies entering articles in the Ladies' Department, and not desiring a ticket of general admission, may have the privilege of entering said articles free.

V.

All applications for space must be made on or before the 26th day of August, on the printed blank forms, which will be furnished by the Secretary, and applicants after that date will not be allotted space until those entered by the 26th of August have been assigned.

Applications for space must state the exact amount and kind required, and for machinery, show cases, etc., a plan of the floor, counter, or wall space must accompany the application.

Space allotted to applicants, and not occupied by them on or before the day of public opening, may be assigned to other exhibitors. And the Board reserve the right to exclude from the Exposition patent medicines, nostrums, and articles of an explosive, highly inflammable, dangerous, or offensive character; also, articles presented after the day of public opening, when the same can not be introduced into the Exposition without undue inconvenience to other exhibitors and visitors. Whenever the articles will admit, contributors are requested to exhibit them in glass cases.

VI.

Exhibitors will be furnished by the Entry Clerk with duplicate cards, describing each article entered for exhibition; these will be countersigned on the receipt of the articles into the Exposition. One of these cards shall be conspicuously attached to the article which it describes, and the other must be retained by the exhibitor, and be presented as his order for the delivery of the article specified, at the close of the Exposition.

VII.

Judges in each class, to pass upon the merits, etc., of the articles entered for competition, shall be appointed as follows: One by the Board, one by the exhibitors in competition in each class, and the third by the two thus chosen.

They shall be men wholly disinterested, and eminent for their skill and experience in the class of articles assigned to them.

VIII.

Machines, and other articles exhibited for premium, will be subjected, where practicable, to thorough tests to determine their efficiency, economy, or other alleged merits. And in this respect it is the purpose of the Board to conduct the Exposition in such a manner that its action, in every case, will command the confidence of the public.

IX.

The premium list will be published, and all awards shall be for the *first degree of merit in each class.* No second class awards or decisions will be made or reported in any case, *excepting in the Fine Arts and Horticultural Departments.*

X.

The main line of shafting, from which power will be furnished for machinery in operation, is 2 7-16 inches in diameter, and will be run at the speed of 200 revolutions per minute. Driving pulleys of any required diameter, also counter shafts and pulleys, and belts and hangers, will be furnished to exhibitors at cost, if timely arrangements for them are made. Pulleys for the main line of shafting, if furnished by exhibitors, must be accurately balanced, and must have the exhibitor's name plainly marked upon them, and should be received before the 26th of August, to enable them to be put in place on the shaft without unnecessary labor and inconvenience.

XI.

No article on exhibition can be removed from the premises during the Exposition. But all appropriate facilities for making sales of articles for delivery at the close of the Exposition will be afforded.

XII.

An adequate police force will be in attendance upon the premises during the day, and watchmen at night; but all articles on exhibition will be at the risk of the owner. Insurance against loss by fire will be effected by the Board in behalf of all exhibitors who apply and provide for the same.

XIII.

In order to preserve the general harmony of the Exhibition, and to make the display of goods symmetrical and attractive, the Board reserve the right to direct the general arrangement of all articles on exhibition, and to regulate the dimensions of all signs and advertisements.

XIV.

Exhibitors may procure employes' tickets at two dollars each, when shown to the President that the *general admission of such employe is absolutely necessary for the care of the exhibitor's articles;* but not more than one of such tickets will be issued to an exhibitor, unless by permission of the Board of Commissioners. Applications for employes' tickets must be made in writing to the President, stating the necessity for the application.

Employes' tickets found to be unnecessary for the purpose for which they were issued, will be forfeited.

All tickets of general admission will be registered, and taken up and forfeited if presented by any other person than the party to whom they were issued.

[NOTE.—The great abuse in the use of exhibitors', and especially of employes' tickets during former Expositions, compels the Commissioners to adopt stringent rules for their government, which will be rigidly enforced.]

XV.

All communications relating to the Exposition, and all boxes or packages containing articles for the Exposition, should be directed to " CINCINNATI INDUSTRIAL EXPOSITION," CINCINNATI, *with the name and residence of the sender plainly marked thereon.* A detailed statement of the contents of each box or package should be inclosed with the same, and a duplicate sent by mail, with full instructions as to whether the exhibitor's agent will take charge of the articles, or the Exposition Board have the package opened and the goods placed on exhibition.

CINCINNATI

Industrial Exposition,

1872.

———⊶•⊷———

PREMIUM LIST.

The management of the Cincinnati Industrial Exposition for 1872 will award the following list of premiums, all of which shall be of the *first degree*, except as stated in the Art and Horticultural Departments. All articles not specifically named in the published list of premiums will be placed on exhibition only, and will be afforded every opportunity for display and advertisement.

Articles named in the premium list may be entered for exhibition only, if the exhibitor so desires.

Articles for competition must be of American manufacture or production, and entered in the name of the manufacturer or producer, or their authorized agent, *except the articles marked with an asterisk* (*), which will not be required to be of American manufacture or to be entered in the name of the manufacturer or producer.

The judges appointed to pass upon the merits of the competing articles will be instructed to place, during the last week of the Exposition, a premium badge prominently on the article to which they have made an award.

The Board of Commissioners will not open the reports of judges until after the premium badges have been placed.

THIRD

CINCINNATI INDUSTRIAL EXPOSITION, 1872.

Classified Premium List.

DEPARTMENT A.

MACHINERY.

Class No. 1.

STEAM ENGINES, BOILERS, STEAM PUMPS, STEAM HAMMERS, AND ALL APPARATUS OPERATED DIRECTLY BY STEAM.

No. OF PREMIUM.   FIRST PREMIUM.

1. Best Automatic Cut-off Stationary Steam Engine. (This premium is given to promote the introduction of a class of Steam Engines calculated to reduce the *consumption of fuel.*).................................Gold Medal.
2. " Smoke Consuming Steam Boiler Furnace............Silver Medal.
3. " Stationary Saw Mill Engine.................................. "   "
4. " Portable Saw Mill Engine.. "   "
5. " Vertical Boiler and Engine combined....................Bronze Medal.
6. " Reversible Steam Engine for Hoisting Purposes, etc. "   "
7. " Steam Pump, Direct Action...................................Silver Medal.
8. " Steam Pump, with Crank and Fly-wheel..............Bronze Medal.
9. " Independent Boiler Feeder..................................... "   "
10. " Automatic Boiler Feeder....................................... "   "
11. " Steam Hammer...Silver Medal.
12. " Rotary Steam Engine... "   "
13. " Traction or Road Engine.. "   "
14. " Portable Farm Engine...Bronze Medal

Class No. 2.

STEAM BOLER AND ENGINE FITTINGS, INCLUDING GOVERNORS, SAFETY VALVES, STEAM GAUGES, WATER GAUGES, LOW AND HIGH WATER ALARMS, GRATE BARS AND APPLIANCES.

No. of Premium.   First Premium.

15. Best Low Water Indicator for Steam Boilers..................Silver Medal.
16. "   Steam Gauge...   "   "
17. "   Safety Valve for Steam Boilers............................Bronze Medal.
18. "   Steam Engine Governor...................................Silver Medal.
19. "   Combined Heater and Lime Extractor for Steam
            Boilers..   "   "
20. "   Tallow Lubricator for Steam Cylinders..................Bronze Medal.
21. "   Piston Packing..   "   "

Class No. 3.

TURBINE WATER WHEELS AND OTHER HYDRAULIC MACHINERY, EXCLUSIVE OF STEAM PUMPS.

22. Best Double-acting Lift and Force Pump for General
           Purposes..Silver Medal.
23. "   Water Pressure Engine...   "   "
24. "   Centrifugal Pump...Bronze Medal.
25. "   Rotary Pump..   "   "
26. "   Cistern Pump..   "   "
27. "   Screw or Propeller Pump...................................Silver Medal.
28. "   Fire Hydrants..Bronze Medal.
29. "   Water Meter.......................... ....Silver Medal.
30. "   Tank Valve for Railroad Water Stations.................   "   "
31. "   Hydraulic Press..   "   "

(Turbine Water Wheels have been omitted from this Premium List, owing to the impracticability of making satisfactory tests.)

Class No. 4.

ELECTRIC ENGINES, AIR AND CALORIC ENGINES, GAS ENGINES, ANIMAL POWERS, AND ALL OTHER MOVERS OR MOTIVE POWER NOT INCLUDED IN CLASSES 1 AND 3.

32. Best Electric Engine, Motor for Light Work...............Silver Medal.
33. "   Caloric Engine, Motor for Light Work..................   "   "
34. "   Gas Engine, Motor for Light Work.....................Bronze Medal.
35. "   Horse Power...   "   "

Class No. 5.

MACHINISTS' TOOLS AND GENERAL METAL WORKING MACHINERY.

No. OF PREMIUM.   FIRST PREMIUM.

36. Best Railroad Car-wheel and Axle Machinery............Gold Medal.
37. "   Engine Lathe...Silver Medal.
38. "   Planing Machine..Bronze Medal.
39. "   Upright Drilling Machine................................ "   "
40. "   Radial Drilling Machine................................Silver Medal.
41. "   Boring and Turning Mill................................ "   "
42. "   Shaping Machine.. "   "
43. "   Bolt or Screw Cutter.....................................Bronze Medal.
44. "   Power Shearing and Punching Machinery.............Silver Medal.
45. "   Stove Pipe Elbow Machine.............................. "   "
46. "   Ratchet Drill..Bronze Medal.
47. "   Boiler Flue Expander.................................... "   "
48. "   Assortment of Tinner's Tools...........................Silver Medal.
49. "   Nail Machine.. "   "
50. "   Tack Machine... "   "
51. "   Pin Machine.. "   "
52. "   Lead Pipe Machine .... "   "

Class No. 6.

WOOD-WORKING MACHINERY.

53. Best Band Saw for Lumber. (This premium is given to
         promote the introduction of *Machinery* calculated
         to lessen the waste in sawing expensive lumber.)..Gold Medal.
54. "   Band Saw for Scroll Work................................Silver Medal.
55. "   Reciprocating Saw for Scroll Work. ....Bronze Medal.
56. "   Variable Stroke Mortiser..................................Silver Medal.
57. "   Hub Mortising Machine...................................Bronze Medal.
58. "   Bung Machinery..Gold Medal.
59. "   Barrel Machinery...Silver Medal.
60. "   Lathe for Irregular Forms................................ "   "
61. "   Stave Machine..Bronze Medal.
62. "   Carving and Frizzing Machine...........................Silver Medal.
63. "   Hoop Machine.. "   "
64. "   Tennoning Machine.......................................Bronze Medal.
65. "   General Wood-working Machine.......................Silver Medal.
66. "   Molding Machine... "   "
67. "   Dovetailing Machine..................................... "   "
68. "   Blind Slat Tennoning Machine.........................Bronze Medal.
69. "   Flooring Machine.. "   "
70. "   Blind Wiring Machine................................... "   "
71. "   Machine for Dressing Timber............................Silver Medal.

Class No. 7.

PRINTING, STEREOTYPING, LITHOGRAPHING, ENGRAVING, BOOK-BINDING, AND TAG MACHINERY, WITH APPLIANCES, MATERIALS, AND SAMPLES.

No. of Premium.   First Premium.

72. Best Stop Cylinder Printing Press ....Silver Medal.
73. " Platen Printing Press................................ "   "
74. " Type Casting Machine................................Bronze Medal.
75. " Assortment Book-binding Machinery...............Silver Medal.
76. " Tag Machinery... "   "
77. " Lithographic Printing Machine...................... "   "
78. " Engraving Printing Machine......................... "   "
79. " Consecutive Numbering Machine.................... "   "

Class No. 8.

SEWING MACHINES.

By special request, no premiums will be awarded in this class.

Class No. 9.

COTTON, WOOLEN, PAPER, HEMP, AND RAG MACHINERY.

80. Best Cotton Gin ....Silver Medal.
81. " Cotton Press.. "   "
82. " Cotton Seed Huller................................... "   "
83. " Cotton Picker and Lapper........................... "   "
84. " Cotton or Wool Carding Machine................... "   "
85. " Cotton or Wool Spinning Machine.................. "   "
86. " Waste Machine for Wool Clippings................Bronze Medal.
87. " Knitting Machine....................................Silver Medal.
88. " Hand Loom... "   "
89. " Power Loom... "   "
90. " Paper Machinery...................................... "   "
91. " Paper Bag Machine .... "   "
92. " Machine for Making Clothing Card................ "   "

Class No. 10.

DISTILLING AND RECTIFYING MACHINERY AND PROCESSES.

By special request, no premiums will be offered in this class.

Class No. 11.

PRESSURE BLOWERS, POWER FANS, BELLOWS, AIR PUMPS, ETC.

93. Best Power Pressure Blower............................Silver Medal.
94. " Power Fan Blower..................................... "   "
95. " Hand Blacksmith Blower ....Bronze Medal.
96. " Blacksmith's Bellows................................ "   "

Class No. 12.

HOISTING MACHINERY.

| No. of Premium. | First Premium. |

97. Best Hydraulic Hoisting Machine ....Silver Medal.
98. " Steam Power Hoisting Machine............................. " "
99. " Hand Hoisting Machine...................................Bronze Medal.

Class No. 13.

BOOT, SHOE, AND LEATHER MACHINERY.

100. Best Sole Stitching Machine for Boots and Shoes............Silver Medal.
101. " Sole Cutting Machine for Boots and Shoes.............. " "
102. " Power Pegging Machine for Boots and Shoes.......... " "
103. " Hand Pegging Machine for Boots and Shoes .... " "
104. " Assortment of Boot and Shoe Machinery .... " "

Class No. 14.

WASHING MACHINES, WRINGERS, CRIMPING MACHINES, MANGLES, IRONING AND CLOTHES DRYING APPARATUS.

105. Best Washing Machine...Bronze Medal.
106. " Roller Wringing Machine...................................... " "
107. " Centrifugal Wringing Machine............................. " "
108. " Crimping Machine... " "
109. " Portable Mangle... " "
110. " Clothes Drying Apparatus................................. " "

Class No. 15.

TOBACCO MACHINERY.

111. Best Tobacco Cutter ....Silver Medal.
112. " Plug Tobacco Machine...................................... " "
113. " Cigar Making Machine.................................Bronze Medal.
114. " Cigar Molds... " "

Class No. 16.

UNCLASSIFIED MACHINERY AND APPLIANCES.

115. Best Carbonic Acid Gas Fire Engine...........................Silver Medal.
116. " Portable Fire Extinguisher................................. " "
117. " Railroad Car Brake.................................Bronze Medal.
118. " Railroad Car Coupling .... " "
119. " Shaft Coupling .... " "
120. " Meat Chopping Machine................................... " "
121. " Emery Wheel Machinery.................................. " "
122. " Pulley Fastening for Shafting .... " "
123. " Pulley Blocks... " "

Class No. 16—*Continued.*

NO. OF PREMIUM.   FIRST PREMIUM.

124. Best Railroad Car Lifter...Bronze Medal.
125. " Railroad Car Springs .... " "
126. " Mining Drill...Silver Medal.
127. " Brick Machine .... " "
128. " Cracker Machinery .... " "
129. " Railroad Switch .... " "

DEPARTMENT B.

AGRICULTURAL MACHINERY.

Class No. 17.

MOWERS, REAPERS, THRESHERS, SEED DRILLS, AND ATTACHMENTS.

130. Best Reaper and Mower Combined ....Gold Medal.
131. " Mower...Silver Medal.
132. " Lawn Mower... " "
133. " Thresher and Separator .... " "
134. " Grain Drill.. " "
135. " Assortment of Reaper and Mower Knives.............Bronze Medal.
136. " Grain Drill with Guano Attachment.....................Silver Medal.
137. " Broadcast Seeder ....Bronze Medal.
138. " Self Raker for Reapers.. .... " "

Class No. 18.

PLOWS, CULTIVATORS, RAKES, MISCELLANEOUS AGRICULTURAL IMPLEMENTS AND
APPLIANCES.

139. Best Cultivator...Silver Medal.
140. " Riding Cultivator................................... " "
141. " Sulky Hay Rake...................................... " "
142. " Hay Tedder.. " "
143. " Corn Planter...Bronze Medal.
144. " Harrow .... " "
145. " Power Corn Sheller.................................. " "
146. " Hand Corn Sheller................................... " "
147. " Portable Hay Press.................................. " "
148. " Hay and Straw Cutter................................ " "
149. " Root and Vegetable Cutter........................... " "
150. " Churn .... " "
151. " Horse Hay Fork...................................... " "
152. " Corn Husker... " "
153. " Bee Hive, with Bees... .... " "
154. " Portable Fence...................................... " "

Class No. 18—*Continued.*

155. Best Assortment of Plows..Silver Medal.
156. " Sulky Plow...Bronze Medal.
157. " Two Horse Plow.. "   "
158. " Steam Plow...Silver Medal.

Class No. 19.

CANE AND CIDER MILLS, AND SUGAR EVAPORATING MACHINERY.

159. Best Sugar Mill......................................Silver Medal.
160. " Sugar Evaporator.................................... "   "
161. " Cider Mill..Bronze Medal.
162. " Sorgo Mill..... .... "   "

Class No. 20.

GRINDING AND FEED MILLS AND GRAIN SEPARATING AND CLEANING MACHINERY, ETC.

163. Best Stationary Grist Mill for Flour...........................Gold Medal.
164. " Portable Corn Mill................................Silver Medal.
165. " Portable Bolting Chest............................ "   "
166. " Smut Machine........................... .... "   "
167. " Hominy Mill..Bronze Medal.
168. " Separator and Grader...............................Silver Medal.
169. " Assortment of Mill Tools...... ....Bronze Medal.
170. " Flour Packing Machine............................. "   "
171. " Bolting Cloth.. "   "
172. " Mill-Stone Feeder and Separater for Corn.............Bronze Medal.
173. " Self-Tramming, Driving and Balance Irons for Mill-
     Stones........ .... "   "

DEPARTMENT C.

IRON, STEEL, METALS, CASTINGS, ETC.

Class No. 21.

IRON, STEEL, SCALES, AND SAWS.

174. Best Plate Steel for Boilers.................................Gold Medal.
175. " Cast Steel..Silver Medal.
176. " Railroad Bar Steel.................................... "   "
177. " Boiler Iron..Gold Medal.
178. " Merchant Bar Iron ....Silver Medal.
179. " Railroad Iron.. "   "

Class No. 21—*Continued.*

No. OF PREMIUM.   FIRST PREMIUM.

180. Best Hoop Iron...Bronze Medal.
181. "   Assortment Wire...Silver Medal.
182. "   Cut Nails...Bronze Medal.
183. "   Wrought Spikes...   "   "
184. "   Assortment of Saws ....Silver Medal.
185. "   Horse Shoes, Machine Made...........................Bronze Medal.
186. "   Horse Shoes, Hand Made...............................   "   "
187. "   Counter Scales...Silver Medal.
188. "   Platform Scales..   "   "

Class No. 22.

BRASS GOODS, CASTINGS, ETC.

189. Best Assortment of Plumbers' Brass Work.....................Silver Medal.
190. "   Assortment of Machinists' Brass Work..................   "   "
191. "   Assortment of Brass Castings............................   "   "
192. "   Assortment of Common Iron Castings.....................Bronze Medal.
193. "   Assortment of Malleable Iron Castings..................   "   "
194. "   Ornamental Fountain.....................................Silver Medal.
195. "   Drinking Fountain..   "   "
196. "   Statuary, Cast Iron ....Bronze Medal.
197. "   Stable Fittings, Cast Iron...............................Silver Medal.
198. "   Ornamental Wrought Iron Work...........................   "   "

NOTE.—*An ample Water supply has been conveyed into the building, for the use of Exhibitors.*

DEPARTMENT D.

RAILROAD SUPPLIES.

Class No. 23.

199.*Best Display of Railroad Supplies...........................Gold Medal.
200. "   Locomotive Head-light...................................Silver Medal.
201. "   Spun Work for Domes, Cylinder Heads, etc.............Bronze Medal.
202. "   Lamps for Passenger Cars...............................   "   "
203. "   Door Locks and Latches for Railroad Cars.............   "   "
204. "   Car Ventilators ....   "   "
205. "   Railroad Heating Stove, Coal...........................   "   "
206. "   Railroad Heating Stove, Wood...........................   "   "
207. "   Car Seat Springs...   "   "
208. "   Freight Car and Switch Padlocks........................   "   "

DEPARTMENT E.

COOKING, HEATING, AND VENTILATING APPARATUS.

Class No. 24.

COOKING AND HEATING STOVES, RANGES, FURNACES, STEAM HEATERS, AND VENTILATORS.

No. of Premium.		First Premium.
209.	Best Coal Cooking Stove	Gold Medal.
210.	" Wood Cooking Stove	Silver Medal.
211.	" Combined Wood and Coal Cooking Stove	" "
212.	" Heating Stove for Coal	" "
213.	" Heating Stove for Wood	" "
214.	" Open Front Stove for Coal	" "
215.	" Parlor Cook Stove for Coal	" "
216.	" Magazine Stove for Coal	" "
217.	" Parlor Stove for Coal	Bronze Medal.
218.	" Parlor Stove for Wood	" "
219.	" School Stove, Ventilating	Silver Medal.
220.	" Cooking Range	" "
221.	" Portable Range	" "
222.	" Hot Air Furnace	" "
223.	" Steam Heating Apparatus	" "
224.	" Range Furniture	Bronze Medal.
225.	" Stove Furniture	" "
226.	" Gas Cooking Apparatus	Silver Medal.

DEPARTMENT F.

BUILDING MATERIALS AND APPLIANCES.

Class No. 25.

BUILDING AND GENERAL HARDWARE

227.	Best Assortment of Door Locks	Silver Medal.
228.	" Assortment of Edge Tools	" "
229.	" Assortment of Malleable Iron Hardware	Bronze Medal.
230.	" Assortment of Wrought Hinges	" "
231.	" Assortment of Wrought Screws and Bolts	" "
232.	" Assortment of Cabinet Hardware	" "

Class No. 25—*Continued.*

No. of Premium.   First Premium.

233.*Best Display of General Hardware..............................Silver Medal.
234.   "   Weather Strips..Bronze Medal.
235.* "   Display of Cutlery...................................   "   "
236.   "   Assortment of Undertakers' Hardware.................Silver Medal.

Class No. 26.

MARBLES, STONE AND IMITATIONS, BRICK, MARBLE AND SLATE MANTELS AND IMI-
TATIONS, AND GRATES, ETC.

237. Best Marble Mantels...Silver Medal.
238. "   Marbleized Iron Mantels...............................   "   "
239. "   Marbleized Slate Mantels..............................   "   "
240. "   Specimens American Marble.............................   "   "
241. "   Specimens Fire Brick, not less than 12................Bronze Medal.
242. "   Specimens Pressed Building Brick, not less than 12...   "   "
243. "   Specimens Artificial Stone............................   "   "
244. "   Specimens Ornamental Stone Work.......................   "   "
245. "   Specimens Ornamental Brick Work.. ....   "   "
246. "   Fire Grates............................. ....   "   "
247. "   Stone Drain Pipe ....   "   "
248. "   Cement Drain Pipe.....................................   "   "
249. "   Ornamental Chimney Tops...............................   "   "
250. "   Iron Burial Caskets.............. ....Silver Medal.
251. "   Wooden Burial Cases..................................   "   "

Class No. 27.

GAS AND LAMP FIXTURES, BRONZES, STEAM FITTINGS, PLUMBING WORK, ETC.

252.*Best Display of Gas Fixtures...............................Silver Medal.
253.* "   Display of Bronzes. ....   "   "
254.* "   Display of Plumbers' Supplies......................... ....   "   "
255.* "   Display of Lamps.......................................Bronze Medal.
256.* "   Gas Chandelier...Silver Medal.
257. "   Plumbing Work..   "   "
258. "   Assortment of Steam Fittings and Fixtures............   "   "
259. "   Lead Pipe and Sheet Lead...............................   "   "

Class No. 28.

TIN, GALVANIZED IRON, AND SHEET IRON, SHEET BRASS AND COPPER WORK, BELLS,
FIXTURES, AND WORK.

260. Best Galvanized Iron Work...................................Silver Medal.
261. "   Copper Work... ....Bronze Medal.
262. "   Tin Work...   "   "

Class No. 28—*Continued.*

No. of Premium.   First Premium.

263. Best Sheet Brass Work ....Bronze Medal.
264. " Bell Fixtures and Work...............................Silver Medal.
265. " Chime of Bells.. "   "
266. " Assortment of Bells...Bronze Medal.

Class No. 29.

FIRE AND BURGLAR PROOF SAFES, BANK AND SAFE LOCKS, ETC.

By special request, no premiums will be offered to this class.

Class No. 30.

CARPENTERS, JOINERS, CARVERS, STAIR BUILDERS WORK, ETC.

267. Best Carving in Wood, for Building Purposes..................Silver Medal.
268. " Vestibule, for Workmanship.................................. "   "
269. " Set Inside Pivot Blinds, for Workmanship.............Bronze Medal.
270. " Set Inside Shutters, for Workmanship.................... "   "
271. " Specimen of Joining, for Workmanship................. "   "
272. " Specimen of Stair Building, for Workmanship........ "   "
273. " Newel Posts, for Workmanship.............................. "   "

Class No. 31.

ORNAMENTAL WINDOW GLASS, SIGN PAINTING, ETC.

274. Best Stained and Ornamental Window Glass..................Silver Medal.
275. " Wheel-cut Ornamental Window Glass....................Bronze Medal.
276. " Ornamental Cut Window Glass............................ "   "
277. " Memorial Window............................. ....Silver Medal.
278. " Specimens of Graining (Woods and Marbles).........Bronze Medal.
279. " Sign Painting on Glass........ .... "   "

DEPARTMENT G.

DOMESTIC MANUFACTURES.

Class No. 32.

BOOTS, SHOES, FINDINGS, LEATHER, MOROCCO, RUBBER GOODS, LEATHER HOSE, BELTING, ETC.

280. Best Ladies and Misses' Machine-made Shoes ....Silver Medal.
281. " Ladies and Misses' Hand-made Shoes.... .... "   "
282. " Men's Machine-made Boots and Shoes..................... "   "
283. " Men's Hand-made Boots and Shoes........................ "   "
284. " Men's Pegged Boots and Shoes............................. "   "

Class No. 32—*Continued.*

No. OF PREMIUM.   FIRST PREMIUM.

285. Best Assortment of Shoe Findings.............................Bronze Medal.
286. " Sole Leather .... " "
287. " Fair Leather... " "
288. " Morocco .... " "
289. " Calf Skins .... " "
290. " Sheep Skins.. " "
291. " Leather Belting ....Silver Medal.
292. " Leather Hose.....................................Bronze Medal.
293. " Improvement in Tanning or Leather Dressing.......Silver Medal.

Class No. 33.

HARNESS, TRUNKS, TRAVELING EQUIPAGE, ETC.

294. Best Set Coach Harness ....Silver Medal.
295. " Set Buggy Harness .... " "
296. " Set Draft Harness... " "
297. " Saddle and Bridle, Gentlemen's ....Bronze Medal.
298. " Saddle and Bridle, Ladies'................... .... " "
299. " Horse Collars .... " "
300. " Trunk, Ladies'......................................Silver Medal.
301. " Trunk, Gents'.. " "
302. " Valise ....Bronze Medal.
303. " Assortment Traveling Equipage .... " "
304. " Assortment Whips.. " "
305. " Improvement in Harness..............................Silver Medal.

Class No. 34.

PICTURE AND MIRROR FRAMES, MIRRORS, ETC.

306. Best Mirror Frames—Design and Workmanship..............Silver Medal.
307. " Picture Frames—Design and Workmanship .... " "
308.* " Display of Mirrors .... " "
309. " Carved Wood Frame....................................... " "

Class No. 35.

MUSICAL INSTRUMENTS.

By request, no premiums are offered in this class.

Class No. 36.

CARRIAGES AND OTHER LAND CONVEYANCE AND ATTACHMENTS, CHILDREN'S CAR-
RIAGES, HOBBY HORSES, ETC.

By special request, no premiums are offered on pleasure carriages. Exhibition limited to 6 pieces.

310. Best Platform Spring Double Wagon ....Silver Medal.
311. " Farm Wagon ....Bronze Medal.
312. " Omnibus ....Silver Medal.
313. " Street Railroad Car.. " "
314. " Hearse .... " "

Class No. 36—*Continued.*

No. of Premium.   First Premium.

315. Best Wagon Wheel ....Bronze Medal.
316. "   Buggy Wheel...   "   "
317. "   Double Perch for Carriages...................................   "   "
318. "   Carriage Springs and Axles ....   "   "
319. "   Child's Carriage..Silver Medal.
320. "   Hobby Horse...Bronze Medal.
321.* "   Display of Saddlery Hardware ....   "   "

Class No. 37.

TOBACCO LEAF AND MANUFACTURED CIGARS, SNUFF, ETC.

322. Best Hogshead Leaf Tobacco...................................Silver Medal.
323. "   Fine Cut Chewing Tobacco.................................   "   "
324. "   Assortment Plug Tobacco ....   "   "
325. "   Smoking Tobacco ....   "   "
326. "   Cigars from American Tobacco.............................   "   "
327. "   Cigars from Foreign Tobacco..............................   "   "
328. "   Cigars from American and Foreign Tobacco...........   "   "
329. "   Assortments of Snuffs ....Bronze Medal.

Class No. 38.

CURED MEATS, GROCERIES, FLOUR, CRACKERS, ETC.

330. Best Sugar Cured Hams (not less than 6).......................Silver Medal.
331. "   Refined Lard...   "   "
332.* "   Display of Groceries..   "   "
333. "   Barrel Flour...   "   "
334. "   Assortment of Crackers ....   "   "

Class No. 39.

CONFECTIONERY, CANNED FRUIT, JELLIES, PICKLES, ETC.

335. Best Ornamental Confectionery...................................Silver Medal.
336. "   Fine Candies ....   "   "
337. "   Plain Candies ....   "   "
338. "   Chocolate Candies ....Bronze Medal.
339. "   Dragé Candies..   "   "
340. "   Gum Work Candies..   "   "
341. "   Assortment Canned Fruits ....Silver Medal.
342. "   Assortment Jellies...Bronze Medal.
343. "   Assortment Pickles ....   "   "

Class No. 40.

WINES.

344. Best Sparkling Catawba Wines...................................Silver Medal.
345. "   Sparkling Delaware Wines.................................   "   "
346. "   Still Catawba Wines ....   "   "
347. "   Still Delaware Wines ....   "   "
348. "   Still Ives Seedling Wines ....   "   "
349. "   Still Concord Wines ....   "   "
350. "   Still Virginia Seedling Wines ....   "   "

Class No. 41.

BOOKS, STATIONERY, PRINTING, BINDING, ETC.

No. of Premium.   First Premium.

351. Best Fine Book Printing............ ....Silver Medal.
352.   "   School Book Printing..................................   "   "
353.   "   Ornamental Printing.................................. ...... Bronze Medal.
354.   "   Book Binding in full Morocco or calf.....................Silver Medal.
355.   "   Book Binding in half Morocco or calf....................   "   "
356.   "   Book Binding in Cloth..............................Bronze Medal.
357.   "   Blank Books Ruling and Binding.....................Silver Medal.
358.   "   Writing Papers...................................   "   "
359.   "   News Paper................. ....Bronze Medal.
360.   "   No. 1 Book Paper, White.............................   "   "
361.   "   No. 2 Book Paper, White.............................   "   "
362.   "   Tinted Book Papers...................................Silver Medal.
363.   "   Manilla Papers......................................Bronze Medal.
364.   "   Straw Wrapping Papers.............................   "   "

DEPARTMENT H.

OF THE HOUSEHOLD.

Class No. 42.

FURNITURE AND UPHOLSTERY, BILLIARD TABLES, CARPETS, RUGS, MATS, OIL
CLOTHS, ETC.

365. Best Set of Furniture (Design and Workmanship con-
         sidered) ....Gold Medal.
366.   "   Set of Parlor Furniture.................................Silver Medal.
367.   "   Set of Parlor Furniture (Oiled Walnut and Hair
         Cloth)..   "   "
368.   "   Set of Bed Room Furniture..........................   "   "
369.   "   Set of Dining Room Furniture.......................   "   "
370.   "   Set of Library Furniture...........................   "   "
371.   "   Sideboard..Bronze Medal.
372.   "   Office Furniture....................................   "   "
373.   "   Library Table......................................   "   "
374.   "   Easy Chair..   "   "
375.   "   Book Case...   "   "
376.   "   Extension Lounge..................................   "   "
377.   "   Hat Rack..   "   "
378.   "   Etegere...   "   "
379.   "   Assortment of Wood Seat Chairs......................Silver Medal.
380.   "   Assortment of Cane Seat Chairs.....................   "   "
381.   "   Assortment of Upholstered Chairs...................   "   "

Class No. 42—*Continued.*

382. Best Assortment of School Furniture..............................Silver Medal.
383.   "   Billiard Table (Beauty of Design, Finish, and Accu-
racy of Cushions considered)...............................   "   "
384.   "   Set Billiard Balls...Bronze Medal.
385.   "   Spring Mattress........................... ....   "   "
386.   "   Folding Mattress..   "   "
387.   "   Spring Bed Bottom...   "   "

Class No. 43.

PAPER HANGINGS, DECORATIONS, WINDOW SHADES, PAPIER MACHE, ETC.

388.* Best Display of Paper Hangings...................................Bronze Medal.
389.   "   Specimen of Decoration in Paper Hangings, etc......Silver Medal.
390.*   "   Display of Papier Maché......................................Bronze Medal.
391.   "   Window Shades..   "   "
392.   "   Window Shade Fixtures.. ....   "   "
393.*   "   Display Lace Window Curtains and Trimmings......   "   "

Class No. 44.

REFRIGERATORS, WATER COOLERS, FREEZERS, FILTERS, AND MISCELLANEOUS
HOUSE FURNISHING GOODS.

394. Best Refrigerator and Water Cooler Combined...............Silver Medal.
395.   "   Refrigerator... ....   "   "
396.   "   Water Cooler...Bronze Medal.
397.   "   Filter...   "   "
398.   "   Japanned Ware...Silver Medal
399.   "   Retinned Stamped Ware..................................Bronze Medal.
400.   "   Planished Tin Ware..   "   "
401.   "   Ice Cream Freezer..   "   "
402.*   "   Display of House Furnishing Goods.......................Silver Medal.

Class No. 45.

CHINA, GLASS, EARTHENWARE, ETC.

403. Best Assortment of Glassware.......................................Silver Medal.
404.   "   White Granite Ware.......................................   "   "
405.   "   Cream Color Ware...   "   "
406.   "   Yellow and Rockingham Ware............................Bronze Medal.
407.*   "   Display Parian Marble Ware..............................   "   "
408.*   "   Display Glass, China, Porcelain, and Fancy Ware...Silver Medal.

Class No. 46.

WOODEN AND WILLOW WARE, COOPERAGE, WIRE GOODS, BRUSHES, ETC.

409. Best Assortment of Wooden Ware...............................Silver Medal.
410   "   Assortment of Willow Ware.................................Bronze Medal.

NO. OF PREMIUM.   FIRST PREMIUM,
411. Best Assortment of Wire Goods.................................Silver Medal.
412. "   Assortment of Brushes...   "   "
413. "   Beer Cask...Bronze Medal.
414. "   Beer Keg...   "   "
415. "   Well Bucket...   "   "
416. "   White Lead Kegs...   "   "
417. "   Packing Boxes...   "   "
418. "   Tobacco Boxes...   "   "

DEPARTMENT I.

CHEMICALS, DRUGS, APPARATUS. AND APPLIANCES.

Class No. 47.

CHEMICALS, DRUGS, PHARMACEUTICAL PREPARATIONS, PAINTS, OILS, DYE
STUFFS, SOAPS, CANDLES, BAKING POWDER, YEAST PREPARATIONS, ETC.

419. Best Assortment of Chemicals...............................Silver Medal.
420. "   Assortment of Druggists' Glassware and General
           Furnishing Material............................   "   "
421. "   Assortment of Fine and Rare Chemicals.............   "   "
422. "   Assortment of Pharmaceutical Preparations.........   "   "
423. "   Disinfectants and Antiseptics....................   "   "
424. "   Glycerine..   "   "
425. "   Oil of Vitriol and other heavy Acids.....................Bronze Medal.
426. "   Dye Stuffs and Chemicals used in Coloring.............   "   "
427. "   Photographic Chemicals...........................   "   "
428. "   Fruit Essences and Flavoring Extracts.................   "   "
429. "   Glue...   "   "
430. "   Writing Fluid....................................   "   "
431. "   Baking Powder....................................   "   "
432. "   Assortment of Spices.............................   "   "
433. "   Yeast Preparations...............................   "   "
434. "   Assortment of Toilet Soaps.......................   "   "
435. "   Assortment of Staple Soaps.......................   "   "
436. "   Assortment of Laundry Soaps......................   "   "
437. "   Assortment of Perfumery..........................   "   "
438. "   Star Candles...Silver Medal.
439. "   Tallow Candles.......................................Bronze Medal.
440. "   Starch...Silver Medal.
441. "   Plumbago for Lubricating Purposes....................Bronze Medal.
442. "   Black Lead Crucibles..............................   "   "
443. "   Stove Polish......................................   "   "
444. "   Sealing Wax.......................................   "   "

Class No. 48.

SODA WATER APPARATUS, GENERATORS, BOTTLING APPARATUS AND APPLIANCES.

No. OF PREMIUM.   FIRST PREMIUM.
445. Best Soda Water Generating Apparatus.........................Silver Medal.
446. "   Soda Water Draught Apparatus...........................   "   "
447. "   Bottling Apparatus......................................Bronze Medal.

DEPARTMENT K.

SCIENTIFIC.

Class No. 49.

PHILOSOPHICAL, MATHEMATICAL, PHOTOGRAPHIC, OPTICAL, AND TELEGRAPHIC AP-
PARATUS AND APPLIANCES.

448. Best Set Surveyor's Instruments............................Silver Medal.
449. "   Set Drawing Instruments................................Bronze Medal.
450. "   Display of Optical Instruments.........................   "   "
451. "   Telegraphic Instrument for private use...............Silver Medal.
452. "   Saccharometer..Bronze Medal.
453.* "   Display Philosophical Apparatus........................   "   "
454. Greatest Improvement in Telegraphy...........................Silver Medal.
455. Best Lightning Rod...Bronze Medal.
456. "   Burglar Alarm Telegraph..................................   "   "
457. "   Electric Gas Lighter....................................Silver Medal.

Class No. 50.

SURGICAL AND DENTAL INSTRUMENTS AND APPLIANCES, ARTIFICIAL LIMBS, TEETH,
DENTISTRY, ETC.

458. Best Assortment of Surgical Instruments......................Silver Medal.
459. "   Assortment of Dental Instruments........................   "   "
460. "   Artificial Limbs..Bronze Medal.
461. "   Artificial Teeth..Silver Medal.
462. "   Specimen of Dentistry...................................Bronze Medal.
463. "   Assortment of Instruments for Deformities.............Silver Medal.
464. "   Assortment of Artificial Eyes...........................Bronze Medal.

Class No. 51.

MILITARY GOODS, FIRE ARMS, SPORTING APPARATUS, SEAL PRESSES, STAMPS, STEN-
CILS, ETC.

465. Best Assortment of Fire Arms and Hunting Apparatus...Silver Medal.
466.* "   Assortment of Military Goods............................Bronze Medal.

Class No. 51—*Continued.*

No. of Premium.   First Premium.

467. Best Assortment of Regalias..Bronze Medal.
468. "   Stamps and Brands...   "   "
469. "   Seal Presses..   "   "
470. "   Stencil Plates...   "   "

Class No. 52.

WATCHES, CLOCKS, AND OTHER REGISTERING AND SIGNAL APPARATUS; SILVER,
SILVER-PLATED, AND BRITANNIA WARE; JEWELRY, GOLD PENS, PENCILS, ETC.

471. Best Silver Ware, Design and Workmanship...............Silver Medal.
472. "   Plated Ware, Design and Workmanship..................   "   "
473. "   Samples of General Plating........ ....   "   "
474.* "   Display of Clocks..Bronze Medal.
475.* "   Display of Watches...   "   "
476. "   Britannia Ware...   "   "
477. "   Gold Pens, Pencils, and Cases..............................Silver Medal.
478. "   Gold Watch Cases..   "   "
479.* "   Display of Jewelry...   "   "
480. "   Assortment of Imitation Jewelry...........................   "   "

DEPARTMENT L.

TEXTILE FABRICS.

Class No. 53.

WOOLENS AND WOOLEN MIXTURES.

481. Best 3-4 or 6-4 Plain or Double & Twist Cassimeres (not
          less than 5 pieces each of Fancy or Mixed, and of
          Plain Coatings)..Gold Medal.
482. "   Black or Colored all-wool Broadcloth...............Silver Medal.
483. "   Moscow Beaver in wool-dyed colors........................   "   "
484. "   Moscow Beaver in piece-dyed colors.......................   "   "
485. "   6-4 Meltons in Indigo Colors................................   "   "
486. "   3-4 or 6-4 Black Doeskins...................................   "   "
487. "   Castor Beavers (not less than 5 pieces, Black and
          Colors, either piece or wool-dyed).....................   "   "
488. "   All-wool Tweeds, as to quality and variety (not less
          than 10 pieces) ....   "   "
489. "   Repellants..   "   "
490. "   Cadet, Green and Indigo Blue Scoured Jeans..........   "   "
491. "   Display of Scoured Jeans, as to color and quality
          (not less than 25 pieces)...............................   "   "

Class No. 53—*Continued.*

No. of Premium.   First Premium.

492. Best Display of Plaid and Fancy Flannels, as to color and
quality (not less than 10 pieces)..........................Silver Medal.
493. " Flannels in White and Solid Colors (not less than 10
pieces)... "   "
494. " All-wool Blankets, either White or Colored (not less
than 10 pairs)............... ....Silver Medal.
495. " Wool and Cotton Blankets, either White or Colored
(not less than 10 pairs).................................. "   "

Class No. 54.

496. Best 4-4 Standard Brown Cottons ....Silver Medal.
497. " Medium Brown Cottons .... "   "
498. " Fine Brown Cottons.. "   "
499. " Heavy Bleached Cottons (not over 40 inch)........... "   "
500. " Medium Bleached Cottons (not over 40 inch).......... "   "
501. " Display of Standard Prints (as to quality and variety) "   "
502. " Display of Medium Prints (as to quality and variety) "   "
503. " Display of Ginghams (as to quality and variety)...... "   "
504. " Display of Corset Jeans (as to quality and variety)... "   "
505. " Marseilles Quilts.. "   "
506. " Awning Stripes......... .... "   "
507. " Checks... "   "
508. " Lawns and Percales... "   "
509. " Black and Colored Dress Silks...........................Gold Medal.
510. " Dress Goods, all Wool or Wool and Silk, valued at
over 40c. per yard...................................... "   "
511. " Dress Goods, all Wool or Wool and Cotton, valued
under 40c. per yard....................................Silver Medal.
512. " Cotton Hosiery .... "   "
513. " Woolen Hosiery... "   "
514. " Knit Zephyr Goods (as to quality and variety)........ "   "
515. " Zephyr Yarns... "   "
516. " Sewing and Spool Silks.................................... "   "
517. " Assortment of Buttons and Fancy Wares................ "   "
518. " Beamed Cotton Warps, White and Colored............. "   "
519. " Carpet Warps...Bronze Medal.
520. " Tapestry Carpets and Rugs...........................Silver Medal.
521. " Wilton Carpets and Rugs................................. "   "
522. " Assortment of Ladies' Single and Double Shawls..... "   "

Note.—*It is recommended that the finer descriptions of goods be exhibited
under glass.*

Class No. 55.

523. Best Power Loom Flax Bagging..............................Silver Medal.
524. " Power Loom Hemp Bagging............................... "   "
525. " Power Loom Jute Bagging................................ "   "

Class No. 55—*Continued.*

No. OF PREMIUM.   FIRST PREMIUM.

526. Best Hemp Cordage..Bronze Medal.
527. "   Bale Doubled and Dressed Hemp...........................   "   "
528. "   Iron Cotton Tie...   "   "

Class No. 56.

COTTON.

529. Best Bale of Cotton from any State ....Gold Medal.
530. "   Bale of Cotton from Tennessee..........................Silver Medal.
531. "   Bale of Cotton from Alabama ....   "   "
532. "   Bale of Cotton from Arkansas.................................   "   "
533. "   Bale of Cotton from Mississippi...........................   "   "
534. "   Bale of Cotton from Georgia ....   "   "
535. "   Bale of Cotton from Louisiana.............................   "   "
536. "   Bale of Cotton from Texas ....   "   "

NOTE.—*In addition to the above, the trade proposes to give special money premiums for the best Bales, from each State, particulars of which will be announced hereafter. The date of entry is extended for this special class to November 10th.*

Class No. 57.

HATS, CAPS, AND FURS.

537.* Best Display of Hats and Caps....................... ....Bronze Medal.
538.* "   Display of Ladies' and Gents' Furs.........................   "   "
539.* "   Display of Carriage and Sleigh Robes...................   "   "

Class No. 58.

GENTLEMEN'S AND LADIES' FURNISHING GOODS, TAILORING, ETC.

540. Best Shirts for Gentlemen (style and workmanship).......Silver Medal.
541. "   Dress Cloth Suit for Gents.................................. ...Bronze Medal.
542. "   Business Suit for Gents......................................   "   "
543. "   Assortment of Gents' Tailoring............................   "   "
544. "   Assortment of Boys' Tailoring.............................   "   "
545. "   Dressing Gown (Gents').................... ....   "   "
546. "   Ladies' Corsets ....   "   "
547.* "   Display of Gents' Furnishing Goods......................   "   "
548.* "   Display of Ladies' Furnishing Goods.....................   "   "
549.* "   Display of Umbrellas and Canes.......... ....   "   "

DEPARTMENT M.

LADIES' ARTICLES.

Class No. 59.

MILLINERY, MILLINERY AND STRAW GOODS, DRESS AND CLOAK MAKING, ETC.

550. Best Bonnet—Style and Workmanship.........................Silver Medal.
551. "   Assortment of Millinery...   "   "

Class No. 59—*Continued.*

No. of Premium.   First Premium.
552.* Best Display of Millinery and Straw Goods................Silver Medal.
553.   " Walking Suit, Style and Workmanship................   "   "
554.   " Dress Suit—Style and Workmanship................   "   "
555.   " Assortment of Dressmaking................   "   "
556.   " Cloak—Style and Workmanship................Silver Medal.
557.   " Assortment of Ladies' Wraps................   "   "
558.* " Display of Fancy Dress Goods................   "   "
559.* " Display of Artificial Flowers................Bronze Medal.

Class No. 60.

HAIR WORK, WAX WORK, SHELL WORK, NEEDLE WORK, ARTIFICIAL FLOWERS, LACE EMBROIDERY, PATTERNS, ETC.

560. Best Specimen of Wax Work................Silver Medal.
561.   " Assortment of Wax Work................Bronze Medal.
562.   " Bouquet, Wax Work................   "   "
563.   " Fruit, Wax Work................   "   "
564.   " Pond Lily, Wax Work................   "   "
565.   " Refreshments, Wax Work................   "   "
566.   " Cross, Wax Work................   "   "
567.   " Skeleton Leaves................   "   "
568.   " Specimen Ornamental Shell Work................   "   "
569.   " Assortment of Shell Work................   "   "
570.   " Specimen Needle Work, by Hand................Silver Medal.
571.   " Specimen Needle Work, by Machine................   "   "
572.   " Specimen Tatting................Bronze Medal.
573.   " Assortment of Tatting................   "   "
574.   " Specimen of Hair Work................Silver Medal.
575.   " Assortment of Hair Work................Bronze Medal.
576.   " Wreath, Hair Work................   "   "
577.   " Flower, Hair Work................   "   "
578.   " Embroidery, Hair Work................   "   "
579.   " Artificial Flowers................   "   "
580.   " Picture, Worsted Work................Silver Medal.
581.   " Affghan, Worsted Work................   "   "
582.   " Specimen Worsted Work................Bronze Medal.
583.   " Embossed Worsted Work................   "   "
584.   " Embroidery, Worsted Work................   "   "
585.   " Tidy, Worsted Work................   "   "
586.   " Quilt, Silk Patch Work................   "   "
587.   " Quilt, Calico Patch Work................   "   "
588.   " Quilt, Knitted................   "   "
589.   " Quilt, Design................   "   "
590.   " Specimen Crochet Work................   "   "
591.   " Tidy, Crochet Work................   "   "
592.   " Collar, Crochet Work................   "   "
593.   " Silk Embroidery................   "   "
594.   " Slipper Embroidery................   "   "
595.   " Chenille Work................   "   "

Class No. 60—*Continued.*

No. of Premium.   First Premium.

No.			First Premium
596.	Best	Infant's Embroidery	Bronze Medal.
597.	"	Infant's Outfit	" "
598.	"	Chair Cover	" "
599.	"	Bead Work, Embroidery	" "
600.	"	Specimen Bead Work	" "
601.	"	Set Toilet Mats	" "
602.	"	Handkerchief Embroidery	" "
603.	"	Ornamental Leather Work	" "
604.	"	Feather Work	" "
605.	"	Chemise, Yoke and Sleeves	" "
606.	"	Agricultural Wreath	" "
607.	"	Specimens Gold or Silver Embroidery	" "
608.	"	Assortment of Ladies' or Children's Dress Patterns..	" "

DEPARTMENT N.

NATURAL HISTORY, GEOLOGY, ANTIQUITIES, ETC.

Class No. 61.

GEOLOGY AND MINERALOGY.

609. Best Collection of Minerals from any one State.............Silver Medal.
610.   "   General Collection of Minerals............................ "   "
611.   "   Collection of Fossils from any one formation (accord-
              ing to Dana.).. "   "
612.   "   General Collection of Fossils............................... "   "

ZOOLOGY.

613. Best Collection of Mounted Birds and Animals.............Silver Medal.
614.   "   Collection of Skeletons of Birds' and Animals.........Bronze Medal.
615.   "   Collection of Birds Eggs and Nests................ ...... "   "
616.   "   Collection of Insects and Cocoons......................... "   "
617.   "   Collection of Recent Corals................................ "   "
618.   "   Collection of Live Birds....................................Silver Medal.

Class No. 62.

CONCHOLOGY.

619. Best Collection of Land Shells.............................Silver Medal.
620.   "   Collection of Fresh Water Shells.........................Bronze Medal.
621.   "   Collection of Marine Shells............................... "   "

BOTANY.

622. Best Collection of Botanical Specimens (dried). ....Silver Medal.
623.   "   Native and Foreign Woods................................Bronze Medal.
624.   "   Collection of Marine Plants............................... "   "

Class No. 63.

ARCHÆOLOGY.

No. OF PREMIUM.   FIRST PREMIUM.

625. Best Collection of Relics of Indians and Prehistoric Races
  of America...Silver Medal.

NUMISMATOLOGY.

626. Best Collection of Coins and Medals........................Silver Medal.

DEPARTMENT O.

UNCLASSIFIED ARTICLES.

Class No. 64.

DEPARTMENT P.

FINE ARTS.

Class No. 65.

PAINTINGS IN OIL; WATER-COLORS; MECHANICAL, ARCHITECTURAL, CRAYON, AND
PENCIL DRAWING; ENGRAVING ON STEEL, PRECIOUS METALS, AND WOOD;
WOOD CARVING; GENERAL LITHOGRAPHY.

Paintings in Oil—Four medals of first class (silver); four medals of second class (bronze).

Paintings in Water-Colors—One medal of first class (silver); one medal of second class (bronze).

Architectural and Mechanical Drawing—One medal each first class (silver); one medal each second class (bronze).

Crayon and Pencil Drawing—One medal of first class (silver); one medal of second class (bronze).

Engravings on Steel, Wood, Lithography, and Wood Carving—Steel Engraving, one medal of first class (silver).

Wood Engraving—One medal of first class (silver).

Lithography—Two medals of first class (silver).

Wood Carving—One medal of first class (silver).

Engraving on Precious Metals—One medal of first class (silver).

Class No. 66.

PHOTOGRAPHIC PORTRAITS PAINTED IN OIL; PHOTOGRAPHIC PORTRAITS PAINTED
   IN WATER-COLORS; PHOTOGRAPHIC PORTRAITS; PHOTOGRAPHIC LANDSCAPES;
   PHOTOGRAPHIC ARCHITECTURE.

Photographic Portraits in Oil—One medal first class (silver).
Photographic Portraits in Water-Colors—One medal first class (silver).
Photographic Portraits not Colored—One medal first class (silver .
Photographic Landscapes not Colored—One medal first class (silver).
Photographic Architecture not Colored—One medal first class (silver).

Class No. 67.

SCULPTURES.

Two medals of first class (silver); two medals of second class (bronze).

Class No. 68.

DECORATIVE AND FRESCO PAINTING.

One medal of first class (silver); one medal of second class (bronze).

☞ *In addition to the premiums named in the above-mentioned Classes,
the Managers offer a* GOLD MEDAL OF HONOR *to the best work exhibited for
competition, with the proviso that if, in the opinion of the Judges, no work of
superior merit should be exhibited, this award shall not be made, and the Judges
of the Classes Nos. 65, 66, 67, 68, shall constitute the Committee for this Award.*

NOTE.—*The premiums will be awarded in every case to the artist who pro-
duced the work. The attention of exhibitors is requested to the Special Rules
governing in this department. See Special Circular.*

EXPOSITION MEDAL CERTIFICATES.

The Board of Commissioners have determined to *issue to all Exhibitors
receiving medals,* an engraved certificate, to be denominated *"Exposition Medal
Certificate."*

DEPARTMENT Q.

HORTICULTURAL.

---

1. The Horticultural Hall and grounds will be open for the reception of
plants from August 12 to September 4. The opening ceremony of the Exposition will be held on Wednesday, September 4, and exhibitors will be ex
pected to have their plants in position by 6 o'clock P. M. of that day.

2. Applications for space must be made previous to August 15th, except
for Floral Display, which must be made one day previous to the day set apart
for the respective display. Those for Fruit and Vegetables must be made previous to September 12th, stating number and kind of Dishes and Plates required, which will be furnished by the Exposition.

3. Each exhibitor will be required to pay an entry fee of $2, and will have the privilege upon paying $2 in addition to his entry fee for his articles, of securing a ticket of admission (positively not transferable), which will admit him at all hours to the Exposition. Not more than two exhibitors' admission tickets will be issued to a firm or corporation.

4. Premiums on plants and other articles will be awarded September 5, or as soon thereafter as the judges may be ready to report, except premiums on fruit, vegetables, floral designs, cut flowers, bouquets, etc., which will be awarded on days set apart for the display. There will be four days set apart for floral displays—one day for fruit and vegetables; due notice of which will be given all the exhibitors.

5. All articles offered for competition must be the property of the person in whose name they are exhibited.

6. Plants entered for special premiums will not be allowed to compete for premiums in collections. No collection of flowers or ornamental designs will be allowed to compete for more than one prize. The articles must be marked so as to designate what prizes are competed for, and no second prize shall be awarded to the same person in the same class.

7. Judges shall be appointed on or before the day of public opening, and on or before special exhibition days, as follows: One by the Commissioners, one by the exhibitors in competition, and the third by the two thus chosen, and all shall be persons wholly disinterested.

8. Exhibitors will be allowed to sell bouquets in the Floral Hall, and in such other parts of the Exposition building as may be set apart for that purpose; provided they are sold from suitable flower stands. But in no case will persons be allowed to sell bouquets within the buildings or grounds who are not exhibitors. This rule will be strictly enforced.

9. All plants and flowers entered for competition, either on show days or during the continuance of the Exposition, must be reported to the Committee, and be put at once in their proper positions. All specimens exhibited for premiums must have their names legibly and correctly written and attached to them.

10. No article or plant, or lot of plants on exhibition will be entitled to a premium unless they possess points of superiority, and the judges will be strictly required to withhold rewards if in their opinion the articles or plants do not merit them. The mere fact that there is no competition shall not be considered a sufficient ground for making an award.

11. Qualifying words used in the premium list shall be entitled to preference in the order of their priority.

12. No plants will be permitted to be removed after being arranged and placed in position till the close of the Exposition, except such as are in a perishable condition, or are replaced by other plants; and all exhibitors will be expected and required to replace all perishable plants as much as is in their power.

13. All Fruit and Vegetables offered for competition must be the production of the persons in whose name they are exhibited, and in no case shall Judges or Committees award premiums for articles that are not strictly superior and better than are usually found in market.

14. All Fruits and Vegetables entered for premiums are considered donated to the Exposition.

Class No. 69.

FLORAL DEPARTMENT.

Best Display in Variety and Finest Arrangement—Five Octave, Double
Reed Mason & Hamlin Parlor Organ, awarded by John Church
& Co.—and..$150 00
2d Best Display in Variety and Finest Arrangement........................ 150 00
3d Best Display in Variety and Finest Arrangement 100 00

Best Single Specimen in or out of Bloom..................................... 50 00
2d Best Single Specimen in or out of Bloom.................................. 10 00
Best One Hundred Species—Wheeler & Wilson Family Sewing Ma-
chine, awarded by Wm. Sumner & Co.

Best Fifty Species.. 20 00
Best Twenty-five Species.. 10 00
Best Ten Species.. 5 00

Best Display Variegated Foliage in Variety and Arrangement—Plated
Tea Set, 5 Pieces, awarded by Duhme & Co.
2d Best Display Variegated Foliage in Variety and Arrangement...... 10 00
Best Single Specimen... 10 00

Best Display of Hardy Evergreens... 30 00
2d Best Display of Hardy Evergreens 10 00
Best Single Specimen... 10 00

Best Display of Tropical Evergreens.. 20 00
Best Single Specimen... 10 00

Best Display and Variety of Tub Plants—New Singer Family Sewing
Machine, awarded by Singer Sewing Machine Co.
2d Best Display and Variety of Tub Plants.................................. 20 00
Best Single Specimen... 10 00

Best Display and Variety of Caladiums....................................... 30 00
2d Best Display and Variety of Caladiums................................... 20 00

Best Specimen Caladium Esculentum... 15 00
Best Specimen Caladium Colocasia... 15 00

Best Display of Ferns and Lycopods.. 50 00
2d Best Display of Ferns and Lycopods. 25 00
Best Single Specimen of Ferns... 15 00

Best Display of Cactuses and Aloes.. 20 00
Best Single Specimen Cactus... 10 00
Best Single Specimen of Aloe.. 10 00

Best Collection of Orchids (open to Amateurs)..............................
2d Best Collection of Orchids,   "   "   ....
Best Single Specimen,   "   "   ....

Suitable special awards will be made in this specialty.

Best Collection of New Plants, not less than twelve.......................... $25 00
2d Best Collection of New Plants.. 15 00
Best Six New Plants.. 10 00

Best Display of Begonias.. 25 00
2d Best Display of Begonias... 15 00
Best Single Specimen... 10 00

Best Display of Fuchsias... 20 00
2d Best Display of Fuchsias.. 10 00
Best Single Specimen—China Tea Set, awarded by Mollenhoff & Co.

Best Display of Roses, General Collection,   (in Pots)...................... 25 00
2d Best Display of Roses, General Collection,   "   " 10 00
Best Single Specimen,   "   " 5 00

Best Display of Geraniums, General Collection................................ 30 00
2d Best Display of Geraniums, General Collection............................ 15 00
Best Single Specimen... 10 00

Best Display of Variegated Geraniums.. 10 00
2d Best Display of Variegated Geraniums....................................... 5 00

Best Display of Double Geraniums... 20 00
2d Best Display of Double Geraniums... 10 00

Best Display of Climbers on Globes or Trellises—Plated Water Set,
     Four Pieces, awarded by Clemens Oskamp & Co.
2d Best Display of Climbers on Globes or Trellises........................... 10 00
Best Single Specimen... 10 00

Best Display of Coleus and Achyranthus.... .... 20 00
2d Best Display of Coleus and Achyranthus.................................... 10 00
Best Single Specimen... 5 00

Best Display of Verbenas, not less than twenty-four, named.............. 15 00
2d Best Display of Verbenas.. 10 00

Best Collection of Seedling Verbenas, not less than twelve................ 10 00
2d Best Collection of Seedling Verbenas, not less than twelve........... 5 00

Best Display of Phlox Drummondii... 10 00
2d Best Display of Phlox Drummondii... 5 00

Best Display of Gladioluses,   (in Pots).................................... 10 00
2d Best Display of Gladioluses,   "   " 5 00

Best General Display of Double and Single Petunias......................... 20 00
Best Display of Petunias, Double.. 10 00
2d Best Display of Petunias, Double.. 5 00

Best Display of Petunias, Single... 10 00
2d Best Display of Petunias, Single... 5 00

Best Display of Lantanas... 20 00
2d Best Display of Latanas.. 10 00
Best Single Specimen... 10 00

Best Display of Balsams $15 00
2d Best Display of Balsams.. 10 00
Best Single Specimen... 5 00

Best Display of Asters.. 10 00
2d Best Display of Asters.. 5 00

Best Display of Liliums, in Pots.. 20 00
2d Best Display of Liliums... 10 00

Best Display of Dianthuses and Picotees... 10 00
2d Best Display of Dianthuses and Picotees.. 5 00

Best Collection of Palms, not less than three 30 00
Best Single Specimen... 20 00

Best Display of Pansies... 10 00
2d Best Display of Pansies... 5 00

Best Display of Antirrhinums.. 10 00
2d Best Display of Antirrhinums.. 5 00

Best Display of Chrysanthemums.. 10 00
2d Best Display of Chrysanthemums.. 5 00

Best Display of Zinnias... 10 00
2d Best Display of Zinnias... 5 00

Best Display of Marantas... 20 00
2d Best Display of Marantas... 10 00

Best Display of Cannas.. 15 00
2d Best Display of Cannas.. 10 00
Best Single Specimen... 5 00

Best Collection of Bouvardias.. 10 00
2d Best Collection of Bouvardias.. 5 00

Best Display of Ornamental Grasses.. 20 00
2d Best Display of Ornamental Grasses... 15 00
Best Single Specimen... 15 00

Best Ribbon Bed... 50 00
2d Best Ribbon Bed... 25 00

Best Miniature Landscape, not less than six feet square—Nubian
    Slave Epergne, Flower and Fruit Stand, awarded by Manning &
    Robinson. Open to Amateurs.

Best Design in Rock Work.. 100 00
2d Best Design in Rock Work.. 50 00

Best Design in Living Plants... 50 00
2d Best Design in Living Plants.. 25 00

Best Arch of Living Plants... 25 00
2d Best Arch of Living Plants.. 15 00

All entries for the five preceding Premiums must be made previous to
August 12th, accompanied by Diagrams giving full-size, in order that proper
location may be set apart for the same. This information will be for use of
the Floral Committee, and will be strictly confidential.

Best Collection Everlasting Flowers.. $10 00
2d Best Collection Everlasting Flowers... 5 00

Best Collection Gloxinias... .... 10 00
2d Best Collection Gloxinias.. 5 00

Best Collection Tropæolum.. 10 00
2d Best Collection Tropæolum.. 5 00

Best Collection Odoriferous Plants................... .... 20 00
2d Best Collection Odoriferous Plants... 20 00
Best Specimen.. 5 00

Best Collection of Coxcombs... 10 00
2d Best Collection of Coxcombs... 5 00

Best Specimen Ricinus.. .... 10 00
2d Best Specimen Ricinus................................ .... 5 00

Victoria Regia, Silver Medal.

Best Collection and Display—Premium awarded by J. Shillito, Esq., of 100 00
2d Best Collection... .... 50 00
Best Five Specimens... 50 00
Best Single Specimen—Bronze Statue, (Affectation,) awarded by Wm.
    McGrew & Co.
2d Best Single Specimen.. 15 00

Best Hanging Basket—Majolica Garden Seat, awarded by F. Schultze
    & Co.
    The above six premiums for *Amateurs only.*

Best Wardian Case, filled.. 20 00

Best Four Hanging Baskets, nearest alike, filled................................. 15 00
2d Best Four Hanging Baskets, nearest alike, filled............................. 10 00
Best Pair Hanging Baskets, nearest alike, filled.................................. 10 00
2d Best Pair Hanging Baskets, nearest alike, filled............................. 5 00

Best and Largest Hanging Basket, filled... 20 00

Best Collection of Rustic Work, filled.. 40 00
Best Piece of Rustic Work, filled... 20 00

Best Rustic Vase, filled... 15 00
2d Best Rustic Vase, filled.. 10 00

Best Pair Terra Cotta, or Iron Vases, filled.. 20 00
2d Best Pair Terra Cotta, or Iron Vases, filled.................................... 10 00

Best Collection of Garden Statuary, open to Amateurs, Silver Medal.
Best Marine Aquarium Stocked, Silver Medal.
Best Fresh-water Aquarium, Stocked.. 25 00
2d Best Fresh-water Aquarium, Stocked... 10 00
    All Premiums for Aquariums open to Amateurs.

Best Display in Variety of Floral Work.. 25 00
2d Best Display in Variety of Floral Work... 15 00
Best Single Piece, Silver Medal.

Best Specimen of Floral Work by Lady Amateur—Set Croquet, Donated by Cincinnati Tin and Japan Co.

Best Display of Cut Flowers	$25 00
2d Best Display of Cut Flowers	15 00
Best Display of Cut Roses	15 00
2d Best Display of Cut Roses	10 00
Best Display of Dahlias	20 00
2d Best Display of Dahlias	15 00
Best Twenty-four Varieties	10 00
Best Twelve Varieties	5 00
Best Display of Gladioluses	15 00
2d Best Display of Gladioluses	10 00
Best Twelve Varieties	5 00
Best Basket of Cut Flowers	15 00
2d Best Basket of Cut Flowers	10 00
Best Wreath, Cross, Crown, and Anchor, in Cut Flowers	25 00
2d Best Wreath, Cross, Crown, and Anchor, in Cut Flowers	15 00
Best Pair of Pyramidal Bouquets, not less than fifteen inches high	20 00
2d Best Pair of Pyramidal Bouquets, not less than fifteen inches high,	10 00
Best Pair of Pyramidal Bouquets, eight inches high	5 00
2d Best Pair of Pyramidal Bouquets, eight inches high	5 00
Best Pair of Hand Bouquets, Convex, six inches in diameter	15 00
2d Best Pair of Hand Bouquets, Convex, six inches in diameter	10 00
Best Bride's Bouquet, six inches in diameter	10 00
Best Vase, or Loose Bouquet	10 00
2d Best Vase, or Loose Bouquet	5 00
Best New Design in Floral Work, Silver Medal	
Best Collection of Living Birds, Silver Medal	

To the Exhibitor taking the Greatest Number of Prizes during the Exposition, a Silver Medal will be awarded.

FRUITS AND VEGETABLES.

Class No. 70.

Display held on 18th, 19th, 20th and 21st days of September.

All articles to be in proper place at 2 P. M. on opening day.

Best Display and Variety by any State	Gold Medal.
Best Display and Variety by any County	Silver Medal.
Best Display and Variety by any Township	Bronze Medal.

Best Display and Variety by any individual—Gentlemen's Cabinet Secretary, awarded by Mitchell & Rammelsberg Furniture Co.

APPLES.

Best Display, not less than Twenty Named Varieties, six speci-
mens each.................... ....Silver Medal.

Best Display, not less than Ten Named Varieties, six specimens
each.. $10 00

Best Display, not less than Five Named Varieties, six speci-
mens each.. 5 00

Best Dish, not less than Six Specimens each, of Benoni, Red
Astrachan, Early Harvest, Summer Queen, Fall Pippin,
Gravenstein, Maiden's Blush, Porter, Baldwin, Bellefleur,
Tulpehocken, Hubbardston Nonsuch, King, Northern
Spy, Newtown Pippin, Pryor's Red, Rambo, Rhode Island
Greening, Rome Beauty, Russet, Swaar, Seek-no-Further,
Smith's Cider, Vandevere, White Pippin, each................ 1 00

PEARS.

Collection of not less than One Hundred Named Varieties,
Three Specimens each...Silver Medal.

Collection of not less than Seventy-Five Named Varieties,
Three Specimens each... $25 00

Collection of not less than Fifty Named Varieties, Three Speci-
mens each... 20 00

Collection of not less than Twenty-Five Named Varieties, not
less than Six Specimens each.. 15 00

Collection of not less than Fifteen Named Varieties, not less
than Six Specimens each........ .... 10 00

Collection of not less than Ten Named Varieties, Six Speci-
mens each... 5 00

Best Dish, not less than Six Specimens each, of Beurre Giffard,
Bartlett, Bloodgood, Kingsessing, Tyson, Buffam, Beurre
Bosc, Beurre d'Anjou, Beurre Diel, Beurre Clairgeau, Belle
Lucrative, Dix, Duchesse d'Angouleme, Doyenne, White
Doyenne, Flemish Beauty, Howell, Louise, Bonne de Jer-
sey, Napoleon, Sheldon, Urbaniste, Eglou Morceau, Law-
rence, Vicar of Winkfield, Winter, Nellie, each................ 1 00

GRAPES.

Best Collection of not less than Three Bunches each, grown
in open air...Silver Medal.

Best Collection of not less than Three Bunches each, Twenty-
Five Varieties, grown in open air........ .... $25 00

Best Collection not less than Three Bunches each, Fifteen Varieties, grown in open air... $15 00

Best Collection not less than Three Bunches each, Ten Varie-
ties, grown in open air.. 10 00

Best Collection of Native and Foreign Grapes in Bunches and
Pots—Wine Set, awarded by D. Kinsey & Co.

Best Dish of not less than Six Bunches each, of Alvey's, Allen's,
Hybrid, Taylor's, Crevelling, Herbemont Norton's Virginia
Union Village, Goethe, Wilder's, Lindley, Agawam, Meri-

mack, Barry's Othello, Cynthiana, Cunningham, Catawba, Delaware, Eumelan, Hartford, Iona, Israella, Ives, Martha, Maxatawney Rebecca, Rentz, Salem, Telegraph, Walter Croton, each.. $1 00

FOREIGN GRAPES.

Three Plants Fruiting in Pots, Best.....................................	$10 00
2d Best.....................	5 00
Ten Cut Bunches, Ten Varieties, Best.................................	8 00
Ten Cut Bunches, Ten Varieties, 2d Best.............................	4 00
Six Cut Bunches, Six Varieties, Best...................................	5 00
Six Cut Bunches, Six Varieties, 2d Best..............................	3 00
Hamburgh, Three Bunches, Best.....................................	3 00
2d Best...	2 00
Best Specimen Bunch, Hamburgh.............................	2 00
Any other dark Variety not less than Three Bunches...............	3 00
Muscat, any Variety, Three Bunches................................	3 00
Specimen Bunch..	2 00
Best New Grape Shown for the First Time, not less than Three Bunches..	5 00

PEACHES.

Collection of not less than Twelve Named Varieties, Six Specimens each..	$10 00
Collection of not less than Nine Named Varieties, Six Specimens each..	5 00
Collection of not less than Six Named Varieties, Six Specimens each..	3 00
Best New Variety, Six Specimens....................................	2 00
Best Dish of Crawford's Early, Crawford's Late, Early York, George the Fourth, Grosse Mignonne, Hale's Early, Heath Cling, Morris White, Oldmixon Free, Oldmixon Cling, Snow, Stump the World, Smock Free, Selby's Cling, Proth's Early, Ward's Late, Gudgeon's Late, each...........	1 00

PLUMS.

Best three Plates (three Varieties, Sweet)...........................	3 00
2d Best three Plates, " "	2 00
German Prune...	2 00
Coe's Golden Drop...	2 00
Duane's Purple...	2 00
Green Gage..	2 00
Minor..	2 00
Damson..	2 00
Wild Goose..	2 00

MISCELLANEOUS FRUITS.

Apricots, Best Display	$3 00
2d Best Display	2 00
Quinces, Best Display	2 00
Watermelons, Best Display	2 00
Other Melons, Best Display	2 00
Best Ornamental Design of Fresh Fruits and Flowers	10 00
2d Best	5 00
Pine Apples in Pots, Three Specimens, Best	10 00
Pine Apples in Pots, 2d Best	5 00
Honey, Best Display	5 00

VEGETABLES.

Potatoes, Best Display	$10 00
Potatoes, 2d Best Display	5 00
Potatoes, 3d Best Display	3 00
Potatoes, Best Peck Early Rose, Climax, Peach Blow, Irish Cup, Early June, White Sprouts, E. Mohawk, each	1 00
Sweet Potatoes, Best Display	4 00
Sweet Potatoes, 2d Best	2 00
Sweet Potatoes, Best Peck	1 00
Parsnips, Best, not less than Twelve Roots	2 00
Parsnips, 2d Best	1 00
Egg Plant, Best Three	2 00
Egg Plant, 2d Best Three	1 00
Carrots, Best Display	3 00
Carrots, Best Twelve Roots	2 00
Carrots, 2d Best Twelve Roots	1 00
Tomatoes, Best Peck	2 00
Tomatoes, 2d Best Peck	1 00
Tomatoes, Best Display in Varieties	4 00
Tomatoes, 2d Best	3 00
Tomatoes, 3d Best	2 00
Cabbages, Best Display, Quality and Varieties	3 00
Cabbages, Best Drumhead, Three Heads	2 00
Cabbages, 2d Best, Three Heads	1 00
Cabbages, Best Savoy, Three Heads	2 00
Cabbages, 2d Best, Three Heads	1 00
Cabbages, Best Red, Three Heads	2 00
Cabbages, 2d Best, Three Heads	1 00
Cabbages, Largest and Heaviest Head	1 00
Broccoli, Best Three Heads	2 00
Broccoli, 2d Best Three Heads	1 00

Onions, Best Display in Varieties............................	$2 00
Onions, 2d Best Display in Varieties............................... ...	1 00
Onions, Best One-half Peck, White..................................	1 00
Onions, Best, Red......	1 00
Beets, Best Long Blood, Twelve Roots..............................	2 00
Beets, 2d Best, Twelve Roots..	1 00
Beets, Best Turnip Blood, Twelve Roots...........................	2 00
Beets, 2d Best, Twelve Roots..	1 00
Beets, Best Sugar, Twelve Roots................................	2 00
Beets, 2d Best, Twelve Roots..	1 00
Salsify, Best, not less than Twelve Roots..........................	2 00
Salsify, 2d Best, Twelve Roots..	1 00
Pepper or Capsicum, Best Display in Variety and Quality......	2 00
Pepper or Capsicum, Best Peck of Mango Peppers.................	1 00
Celery, Best, not less than Three Stalks............................	3 00
Celery, 2d Best, Three Stalks..	2 00
Celery, 3d Best, Three Stalks......	1 00
Celery, Best Half Peck Celeriac...................................... .	1 00
Beans, Snap, Best Half Peck...	2 00
Beans, 2d Best Half Peck	1 00
Beans, Lima, Best Two Quarts, Shelled............................	2 00
Beans, 2d Best Two Quarts, Shelled.................................	1 00
Corn, Best Display in Varieties, Twelve Ears each................	3 00
Corn, 2d Best, Twelve Ears each......................................	2 00
Corn, Best Twelve Ears Field...	2 00
Corn, 2d Best, Field...	1 00
Corn, Best Twelve Ears Sugar...	2 00
Corn, 2d Best, Sugar...	1 00
Corn, Pop..	1 00
Corn, Stalk of Corn with Largest Number of Filled Ears.......	1 00
Squashes, Best Display....................................	4 00
Squashes, 2d Best Display...	2 00
Squashes, 3d Best Display...	1 00
Squashes, for the Largest and Best...................................	2 00
Gourds, Best Display..	2 00
Gourds, 2d Best Display..................................	1 00
Pumpkins, for the Largest and Best	2 00
Pumpkins, 2d Largest and Best..	1 00
Pumpkins, Best Display..	3 00
Pumpkins, 2d Best Display..	2 00
Radishes, Best Dozen..	1 00
Cucumbers, Best Display..	2 00
Cucumbers, 2d Best Display.. .	1 00

Lettuce, Best Six Heads..	$2 00
Lettuce, 2d Best Six Heads..	1 00
Endive, Best Six Heads..	2 00
Endive, 2d Best Six Heads..	1 00
Spinach, Best Display, Half Peck each Sort............................	2 00
Spinach, 2d Best...	1 00
Parsley, Best Three Branches, Curled...................................	1 00
Sweet and Pot Herbs, Best Collection, in Bunches..................	2 00
Sweet and Pot Herbs, 2d Best..	1 00
Turnips, Best Half Peck...	2 00
Turnips, 2d Best.	1 00
Vegetables in Variety, Best Display.....................................	10 00
Vegetables in Variety, 2d Best Display..................................	6 00
Vegetables in Variety, 3d Best Display..................................	4 00
Best Display of Garden Tools.......................................Bronze Medal.	

☞ Fruit and Vegetable List open to Amateurs.

SPECIAL PREMIUM OFFERED BY THE CHAMPION MACHINE COMPANY.—One Champion No. 4 Combined Reaper and Mower, Self-Raker and Dropper. To be awarded by the Exposition for the largest yield of ten acres of wheat grown in Ohio, Indiana or Kentucky, during the year 1872. Competitors for this premium must enter for the same under the rules of the Exposition, and will be required to file with the Secretary an affidavit setting forth the correctness of the measurement of the ground and the yield per acre, which statement must be verified by the affidavit of two responsible parties, and accompanied by a sample of one bushel of the wheat raised on said ground.

THIRD

CINCINNATI INDUSTRIAL EXPOSITION,

1872.

———◦◇◦———

INSTRUCTIONS TO JUDGES.

———◦◇◦———

OFFICE OF THE EXPOSITION,
CINCINNATI, *September*, 1872.

DEAR SIR: You have accepted the position of Judge on Class No. — of the Premium List of Articles entered at the "Cincinnati Industrial Exposition," and I take pleasure in transmitting for your guidance the following instructions.

The Exposition was duly opened to the public on Wednesday, September 4th. The Catalogues will be ready for you on Thursday, September 19th, and you are particularly requested to avail yourselves of every opportunity, both before and after that time, to examine into the merits of the articles belonging to your class, so that you may be able to make a report of your conclusions to the General Committee by Monday, September 30th, at the furthest.

Your attention is particularly called to the printed Rules and Regulations, and more especially to the 7th, 8th, and 9th Rules, which you will please observe in your examinations and decisions, viz:

VII.

Judges in each class, to pass upon the merits, etc., of the articles entered for competition, shall be appointed as follows: One by the Board of Commissioners, one by the exhibitors in competition in each class, and the third by the two thus chosen.

They shall be men wholly disinterested, and eminent for their skill and experience in the class of articles assigned to them.

VIII.

Machines, and other articles exhibited for premium, will be subjected, where practicable, to thorough tests to determine their efficiency, economy, or other alleged merits. And in this respect it is the purpose of the Board to conduct the Exposition in such a manner that its action, in every case, will command the confidence of the public.

IX.

The premium list will be published, and all awards shall be for the first degree of merit in each class. No second class awards or decisions will be made or reported in any case, *excepting in the Fine Arts and Horticultural Departments.*

In making your decisions, it will be necessary, however, for you to exercise a due discretion in regard to articles which, "although the best in their class," are, "from inferiority of design or workmanship, unworthy of any award." In such cases no premiums will be awarded, for it is the aim of this Exposition to stimulate to excellence, rewarding merit only.

You will not permit any interference in your examinations by interested parties or others.

In making the award, your particular attention is called to the following special instructions, viz:

Articles for competition must be of American manufacture or production, and entered in the name of the manufacturer or producer, or by their authorized agent, excepting where otherwise stated in the Premium List.

In displays, the peculiar merit only of the articles will be taken into consideration, with no reference to the number or quantity exhibited.

The judges are requested to hand in their written reports under seal, and these will not be opened by the Exposition Board until the badges have been placed upon the articles awarded premiums.

Your colleague is

and you are requested to appoint immediately the third Judge in accordance with the 7th Rule, and to proceed at once with your examinations.

Any information that you may wish in the furtherance of your duties will be furnished at any time on application at the office.

By presenting this Circular at the door, you will be admitted at all hours until the close of the Exposition. It is, however, not transferable.

Yours, very respectfully,

NOTE.—*The above copy of the Instructions to Judges is printed for the information of the exhibitors, to illustrate the plan of the appointment of the Judges, and the general rules governing them in their examinations and decisions.*

THIRD
ƇINCINNATI JNDUSTRIAL ƎXPOSITION,
1872.

INSTRUCTIONS TO EXHIBITORS.

Office of the EXPOSITION,

CINCINNATI,..., 1872.

DEAR SIR: You, as an Exhibitor in Class No.............of articles included in the published Premium List, are hereby notified that in accordance wi h the 7th Rule of the General Ru'es and Regulations governing the Exposition, it becomes your IMPᴇRATIVE DUTY TO APPOINT THE "SECOND JUDGE," viz:

RULE 7.—"Judges in each class, to pass upon the merits, etc., of the articles entered for competition, shall be appointed as follows: one by the Board of Commissioners, the second, *by the Exhibitors in competition in each class of Premiums,* and the third, by the two thus chosen.

"They shall be men wholly disinterested, and eminent for their skill and experience in the class of articles assigned to them.

"Also, that the Judges appointed to pass upon the merits of competing articles will be instructed to place, during the last week of the Exposition, a Premium Badge prominently on the article to which they have made an award."

You are further notified to attend a meeting of ALL THE EXHIBITO s

IN YOUR CLASS, on ....
promptly, in the "Exhibitors' Room," in the Exposition, for the purpose of appointing said Second Judge.

In order to facilitate the business of the Exposition, said Judge must POSITIVELY BE APPOINTED at the said time and p ace.

The meeting thus convened of the Exhibitors, without reference to what number may be present, WILL BE EMPOWERED to proceed a' once and elect the said Judge, and such action shall be FINAL, and shall not be annulled by the remaining Exhibitors failing to be present at that time

We desire to call your attention to the fact, that the RESPONSIBILITY of having the articles in "YOUR CLASS EXAMINED," and "PREMIUMS AWARDED UPON THE SAME," depends upon the full complement of Judges being appointed.

Any information that you may desire explanatory of the above, or on other subjects in c nnection with the Exposition, will be given cheerfully upon application at this office.

NOTE.—The above instructions are printed for the general information of EXHIBITORS, explanatory of the method adopted for the election of Judges, and also for the purpose of notifying them of their responsibility in having the articles properly examined. Due notice will be given to every Exhibitor to attend the meeting to appoint the "Second Judges."

Fine Arts Department.

The Board of Commissioners recognizing the importance of a higher art culture, both for its own sake and for its influence in the improvement of many of the finer industries, have determined to give this Department special prominence. They have, therefore, with the concurrence of the City Park Commissioners, erected in Washington Park, opposite the main buildings, a large fire-proof hall, to be devoted exclusively to this Department.

It is intended that the collection shall include, in addition to the works of native artists, contributions from private collections in the various classes, and the Board invite the cordial aid of lovers of art in an effort to at once gratify and educate the popular taste for the beautiful.

The divisions embrace works of Painting, Engraving, Sculpture, and Photography. The objects will be catalogued, and every facility given for the sale of works entered for competition.

The Department is in the charge of a committee of experts, and the utmost care will be taken in the handling and repacking of all objects contributed.

All works must be entered between the 1st and 15th of August; and for further information reference is made to the Standing Committee on Fine Arts.

The undersigned, from a personal acquaintance with the gentlemen of the committee, and after an inspection of the building plans, have decided to make contributions from their collections, and cordially unite in the above invitation.

R. R. Springer,	Jos. Longworth,
A. G. Burt,	L. B. Harrison,
Jas. A. Frazer,	Geo. K. Shoenberger,
Wm. Henry Davis,	W. W. Scarborough,
Wm. Karmann,	Geo. H. Pendleton.
W. S. Groesbeck,	

Department of Natural History.

The introduction of the Department of Natural History, which will include geology, mineralogy, conchology, botany, antiquities, etc., is a new feature in the history of Expositions, and the Cincinnati Industrial Exposition has determined to give this most useful and entertaining department the position it deserves.

A cordial invitation is extended to geologists, mineralogists, naturalists, and all others in any way interested in this department, to contribute of their collections, and to enter such specialties as may be of interest to themselves or to the public. The Board of Managers have provided an appropriate fire-proof building, and every facility will be afforded for effective display, and for information to visitors. Contributions sent from a distance will be taken in charge by the committee, placed on exhibition, and returned with care at the close of the Exposition.

Articles entered in this department should be carefully labeled and classified, and when practicable arranged in glass cases.

It is hoped that the liberal opportunity thus offered to establish the department will be attended with complete success.

For further information concerning the department or the premium list, address the Chairman of the Committee.

A. L. HELM,
J. S. NEWBERRY, M. D.
L. S. COLTON,
H. H. HILL, M. D.
JULIUS DEXTER,
Committee.

Horticultural Department.

Owing to the great popularity of this attractive feature of the Exposition of 1871, the Board of Commissioners for the present year have determined to erect a larger and more commodious building, especially adapted to the display of plants, fruits, and vegetables. The display of the past season has never been equaled in the United States, and more space was then demanded by exhibitors than the Floral Hall contained. In order, therefore, to meet every demand, a conservatory has been designed of more than double the proportions of that of 1871. The dimensions of the new structure are 150 by 140 feet; height 45 feet, with clear gallery 150 feet long and 20 feet wide.

For the purpose of preserving the plants uninjured during the continuance of the Exposition, light and ventilation have been fully provided for. The roof and sides will be almost entirely of glass, and capable of being readily opened for ventilation. Three tables, each 140 feet long by 4 feet wide, will be used for the display of fruits and vegetables.

In corresponding liberality, the premium list is the largest and most varied ever offered. Premiums will be awarded for general displays, displays of single kinds in lots, and for single specimens of each and all the leading and favorite plants, fruits, and flowers. Almost every grower of fruits, flowers, and vegetables, by the exhibition of anything truly excel. lent, will thus have the opportunity of competing on equal terms, whether in single specimens or collections. We therefore cordially invite all growers of meritorious specimens to avail themselves of the opportunity thus afforded of exhibiting the products of their knowledge, skill, and taste to the hundreds of thousands who will visit the Exposition.

Particular attention is called to the Gold Medal prize for the best display made by any one State. If more than three entries are made for this premium, a special day will be set apart for the same, in order to give it the prominence which it merits.

The rapidly increasing interest in this department, its advantage and pleasure to both visitors and exhibitors, together with the efforts now being made by the leading horticulturists expressly for this occasion, justify the Board in assuring the public and exhibitors the grandest display in collection and variety ever given in this country.

Cincinnati Industrial Exposition

1872.

FORM OF APPLICATION FOR SPACE.

AMOUNT OF SPACE.

STATE WHETHER WALL, FLOOR, OR COUNTER, OR IF POWER WILL BE REQUIRED.

....

....

....

Applications for space must state the exact amount required, and for machinery, show cases, etc., a plan of the floor, counter, or wall space must accompany the application.

WHAT KIND OF ARTICLES.

....

....

....

....

All articles will be entered for exhibition only, except those specifically named in the published list of articles to which premiums will be awarded, but articles intended for competition must be entered and the Premium competing for stated by the exhibitor at the time of the entry, otherwise they will be entered for exhibition only.

If entered for Premium, fill out from the List the Class and Premium competed for, viz:

Class in the Premium List, - - *No.* ....

Premium Competing for. - - - *No.* ....

.... 1872.

Application for space as above is made by

....

....

....

If entered through an Agent, insert name here:

Per .... *Agent.*

NOTE.—If the Exhibitor is a **non-resident,** he or his representative will please leave his Cincinnati address with the **Entry Clerk,** when entering his articles.